For Mom and Dad, who put up with my tiny tantrums—C. C.

For Hans Christian, Peder August, Ole Jakob—E. O.

tiger tales
5 River Road, Suite 128, Wilton, CT 06897
Published in the United States 2017
Originally published in Great Britain 2017
by Little Tiger Press
Text copyright © 2017 Caroline Crowe
Illustrations copyright © 2017 Ella Okstad
ISBN-13: 978-1-68010-072-3
ISBN-10: 1-68010-072-6
Printed in China
LTP/1400/1826/0217
All rights reserved
10 9 8 7 6 5 4 3 2 1

For more insight and activities, visit us at www.tigertalesbooks.com

TINY TANTRUM

BY
CAROLINE CROWE

ILLUSTRATED BY
ELLA OKSTAD

tiger tales

This is **TINY TANTRUM** when she's getting her own way,
Like eating lots of chocolate cake or when it's time to play.

But you try telling Tiny
that she has to
wash her hair,

Or **tidy up,**

or **go to bed,**

and she'll scream,

"THAT'S NOT FAIR!"

Windows **rattle**, desserts **quake**, and birds **fall** out of trees,

When Mommy dares to say the words,
"Now, put your coat on, please!"

But one day, just as **TINY** stamped
and squeezed her eyes so tight . . .

...a hairy, purple monster gave poor TINY quite a fright!

He said,

"If you don't put your coat on,
then your bottom will get chilly,

And girls with frozen bottoms
can't have fun, you SILLY BILLY!"

"YIKES!" she yelled and grabbed her coat—
"I don't want that at all."
She held the monster's furry paw
and scooted down the hall.

They **kicked** through leaves,
and **climbed** up trees,

and **slid** on icy puddles.

When **TINY** slipped and hurt her knee,
he helped with monster cuddles.

The monster's tummy rumbled, so she took him home to eat.
But when she saw the broccoli, she stamped her **TINY** feet!

Then over by the oven, with a chef's hat on his head,
Stood a monster with an apron on,
and this is what he said:

"When I eat peas or broccoli, I do a little **wiggle**.

Vegetables taste better if you eat them with a **giggle!**"

So **TINY** ate a little bit—she didn't **shout** or **scream**,
And Mommy let them have a bowl of chocolate chip ice cream.

At playtime Molly had the trike, so Tiny opened wide:
"I WANT THAT TRIKE! I WANT IT NOW!"
she screamed 'til Molly cried.

But just as TINY tried to grab,
she heard a whooshing sound.
A monster skidded down the slide
and tumbled to the ground.

He said,

"There are some things
you don't have to share,
like VEGETABLES at lunch,
But sharing toys helps
you stay friends
and maybe
make a bunch."

At bedtime **TINY** and her friends
were bouncing on the bed,
When Daddy said that it was time
to brush her teeth instead.

She clenched her fists and SCREAMED and STAMPED, then, oh, what a surprise!

A monster in pajamas twirled in right before her eyes.

He sang,
"Brushing is exciting!
You don't know what you might find—

Some chocolate or a cookie that got stuck and left behind!"

Now **TINY** is so sleepy, and she wants to go to bed,
But the monsters are still having fun! They want to bounce instead!

"IT'S TIME FOR BED," she says,
but now they squeeze THEIR eyes so tight.

"WE don't want to go to bed! We want to **BOUNCE** all night!"

So Tiny says,

"I'LL COUNT TO FIVE—
YOU'D BETTER SHAKE A LEG!

THE LAST ONE IN
AND COZY IS
A STINKY, ROTTEN EGG!"

"A stinky egg?!" the monsters cry,
and jump right into bed,

Then TINY plants a good-night kiss
on every monster's head.

When **Daddy** comes to say
good night, he doesn't hear a peep.
TINY and her **monster friends**
are tucked in, fast asleep.

Now . . .

...TINY knows the secret, and we'll share it with you, too—
Don't waste your time on tantrums; sing this song we wrote for you!

"Sometimes things seem boring,
and it makes you want to SHOUT,

But don't get cross—
just bend your knees
and SHAKE yourself about.

Give yourself a tickle, dance and sing and **jump** about,

And SOON you'll find you want to let the MONSTER giggles out!"